AGAIN!

To Oliver, Noah, Toby, Ella and Finn

Bloomsbury Publishing, London, Oxford, New York, New Delhi and Sydney

First published in Great Britain in 2017 by Bloomsbury Publishing Plc
50 Bedford Square, London WC1B 3DP

www.bloomsbury.com

ISBN 978 1 4088 8014 2

All papers used by Bloomsbury Publishing are natural, recyclable products made
from wood grown in well managed forests. The manufacturing processes
conform to the environmental regulations of the country of origin

Printed in China by C & C Offset Printing Co. Ltd, Shenzhen, Guangdong

1 3 5 7 9 10 8 6 4 2

AGAIN!

by

Ralph STEADman AGAIN!!

BLOOMSBURY

LONDON OXFORD NEW YORK NEW DELHI SYDNEY

"Hello, Grumpy,"

said Oliver.

"Hello, Oliver,"

said Grumpy.

"What are you doing, Grumpy?"

asked Oliver.

"Nothing really . . ."

"**BOo!**"

replied Grumpy.

"**AGAIN!**"

squealed Oliver.

"How's this?"
said Grumpy.

"What about this?"

"AGAIN!"

"And this?"

" 'AGAIN!' "

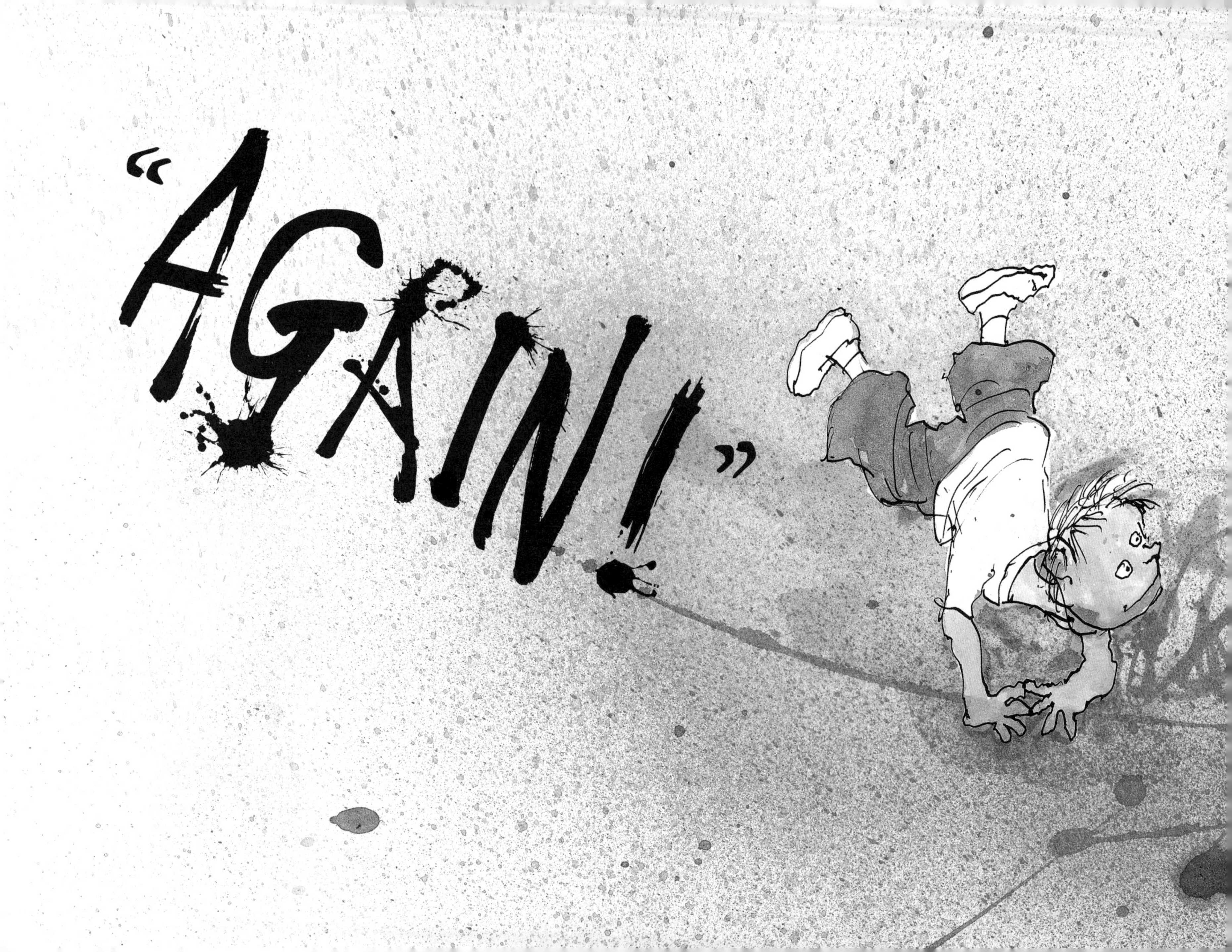
"AGAIN!"

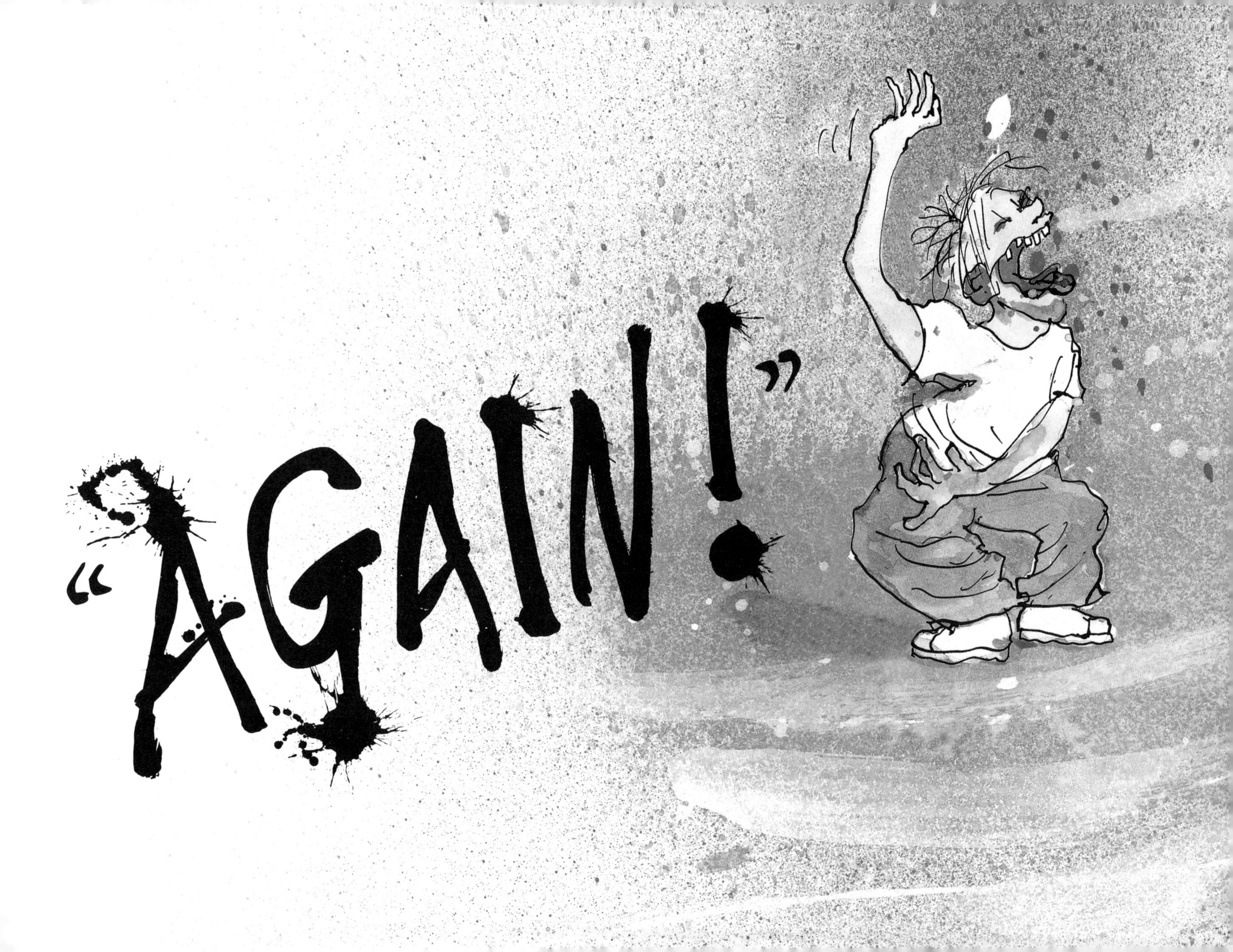
"AGAIN!"

"AGAIN!"

"OK!
This enough?"

"AGAIN . . .

Oh, hello, Noah!"

"Hi Oliver.
What **is** Grumpy doing?"